Property Of:

Illustrated by: Loretta Ford

Edited by: Brittney Rzucidlo

First Edition

ISBN-13: 979-8-9855424-0-0 (Paperback)
ISBN-13: 978-1-7363291-9-1 (eBook)
ISBN-13: 979-8-9855424-9-3 (Hardcover)

Library of Congress Control Number: 2021925899

Typeface: Olde English Regular by Dieter Steffmann

Illustrations designed using Adobe®

This book is dedicated to the memory of Victoria Ann Burgess,
Whose story, unfortunately, ended too soon.
I will forever treasure the time we shared together.

Vicky's Epic Quest

1: Proem

Eladrin's Chapel
Witch's Woods
Burgess Kingdom
Siren Sea
Desolate Desert
Alchemist's Oasis
Palace of Akbar

Sing to me, oh Lord above, of that heroic girl
And of the terrible tragedy which did unfurl.
How lovely Victoria was sent to a far-off land
By her kingly father to secure a prince's hand.
Victoria begged her father not to make her go
And marry someone she did not love or know.
But the king did this to seal a peaceful pact,
Lest by barbaric tribes their realm be sacked.
By swift ship Vicky sailed across the Siren Sea,
Which got its name from the wind's eerie melody.
And so, Victoria and her dowry were sent away,
Sparing her from the evil machinations at play.
Leopold, you saw that you must soon step down
And pass to your son, Henry, that mighty crown.
But, oh great king, this plan will go awry!
For you, wife, and son are fated soon to die.
Your brother, a priest, will play the part!
After demons teach him a most damnable art.
Strange how darkness infects ones once so kind.
Envy and lust for power seized his fragile mind.
Vicky, poor girl, oh the things you will face!
Many dangers await you all over the place.
A crazy uncle and demons straight from Hell,
The sandstorm – oh, and the dragon as well!
But Heaven will send you help on your quest:
An angelic weapon at your mother's request.
And friends shall help you out along the way -
Alas, one will be taken from the light of day.
Listen well, Dear Reader, for I shall tell you how
Because Vicky's Epic Quest begins right now.

2: Eladrin's Lost Soul

Since at this time Vicky is heading to foreign soil,
Let us learn more of her uncle Eladrin's turmoil.
In the valley's green pastures - sure to impress! -
Stands the grand castle of the kingdom Burgess.
But above this city in a snowy mountain pass
There was a lone chapel with ornate stained glass.
In this lonely place the priest, Eladrin, called home.
He had few guests for the pass was unsafe to roam.
Eladrin would often look down at the lush kingdom below,
Yearning for a life his birth order prevented him to know.
Over time the loneliness whispered things in his ear.
Addling his mind with envy, doubt, anger, and fear.
He would not seek help but hid these feelings away.
Until the voices within won out on that fateful day.
Thus, Eladrin lamented and cursed his priestly lot:
"Why, God, give Leo the crown and me jack-squat?!"
Eladrin felt so hurt and cheated by this tragic loss
That over his own knee he snapped the holy cross.
He threw the top of it into the crackling fire
And paced the altar with rage mounting higher.
Tell, Lord, how into darkness his heart was led.
Here was the unholy message, which he said:
"Infernal demons from the depths of Hell,
Come stand before me, I've a soul to sell!"

3: The Cursed Staff

No sooner had the words left his cursed lips,
Than darkness came on like a great eclipse.
As the ground opened to the depths of Hell,
The Devil came forth with a sulfuric smell.
On his left, Judas writhed in terrible pain
As demons lashed him again and again.
On his right, Jezebel, with lust in her face,
Moaned as snakes slid from her every orifice.
Satan approached to take his wretched soul
And in exchange he gave him a magical pole.
As Satan retreated with his new prize,
Eladrin felt pure hatred cloud his eyes.
He wanted to test this scepter's power
By taking the kingdom that very hour.
Rushing down so fast it was like he had flown,
Eladrin soon stood before the king's throne.
Aiming his scepter at his brother's heart,
He uttered a curse and blew the king apart.
Queen Ann and Prince Henry also died that day
And a whole bunch of others who got in his way.

4: A Demonic Feast

In Hell, the minions were called to a meal.
For Lord Satan had a new plan to reveal.
What you ask was the main course of the feast?
Well, it was the soul of that unfortunate priest.
Dear God, protect me as I say each name:
First there was Satan who is all to blame.
To his left sat Lilith, Adam's first wife,
Who caused him and God so much strife.
Now Lilith inhabits a mother's womb,
Seeking to make that place a fetus's tomb.
Rancor squirmed oozing his deadly disease.
He will kill half the realm with dirty fleas.
The Reaper sharpened his scythe with rattling breath -
A chilling noise that often heralds an imminent death.
Ramfalcis was twitching about in his chair;
Impatience called him anywhere but there.
Doldrum slept at the table loudly snoring,
Demon of sloth, who's really quite boring.
Ba'al's chair was currently empty at the other end.
For, he was sent to keep watch on their new friend.
The Berserker twirls his large, two-headed axe.
He loves starting wars — both sides he attacks!
Beelzebub, the arrogant "Lord of the Flies",
Led the fourth crusade after telling the pope lies.
Leviathan, the greatest of all the beasts,
Causes shipwrecks and on the crew feasts!
But all eyes turned to Satan's prized acquisition.
One burned for witchcraft and superstition.

5: The Prophecy

Once upon a time in life healing herbs you often sold.

You also brewed potions and even futures foretold.

But a powerful woman the holy men could not abide.

For you challenged their teachings and hurt their pride.

They said that you blasphemed and called you a "witch"

And that you stole children and husbands did bewitch.

Finally, these men burned you at a stake made of birch.

Even now she harbored deep resentment for the Church.

Thus, this Eladrin she secretly did not want to succeed.

For she believed that all clergy were of the same breed.

Plus, she foresaw the truth would put Vicky in danger

And did not want another girl dead by a priest's anger.

Now the witch was in quite a pickle about what to do.

For, once the prophecy began, she had to speak true.

"Your servant will rule for you throughout every land,

Unless one in a foreign kingdom should take a stand."

Nevertheless, the witch hid a very crucial detail.

In doing this, she hoped Satan's plan would fail.

Satan smiled and joked with them over food

Since recent events put him in a good mood.

Ba'al appeared from the shadows looking grim.

The odds of receiving good news seemed slim.

"Lord Satan may I please have a word?

I've something urgent that must be heard."

"Please Ba'al, I need good news from you today

If you cannot deliver, then you'd best go away."

"But, great master, what of Eladrin's niece?

Only revenge is able to put her soul at peace."

Satan did not think a girl would be a threat,

But her betrothed Akbar? How could he forget!

"Rancor, fetch your most dangerous and deadly disease

To bring this ally of Burgess, Prince Akbar, to his knees.

Ramfalcis and Doldrum, from his city let no one out or in!

Lord Ba'al, swiftly go back to Burgess and protect Eladrin!"

Those demons bowed and departed with haste for the mortal stage.

Now we can leave this infernal place and return to Vicky on the next page.

6: A Sacred Spear

To dear Victoria the ghastly message quickly spread
    That her parents and brother were all truly dead.
    Her hermit uncle seized control but at what cost?
    Eladrin's eternal soul would now be forever lost.
She sought her betrothed to avenge this awful crime
But found Akbar was much too sick at present time.
For, Rancor dripped a nasty disease upon his head,
    Which kept Akbar enfeebled and stuck in his bed.
    Indeed, the prince would have died then and there,
Had the healers not treated him with the utmost care.
    Victoria saw that this was now her chance to flee
    From the marriage, which she never wanted to be.
    Before she fled, she snuck into the palace treasury
And stole an old spear unaware of its holy history.
It was retrieved from a church during some crusade.
By its accursed point, Christ's holy side was flayed.
    With whose very blood, it is given might and luck.
    Indeed, it will find its mark despite a bad chuck.
        With said spear in hand, she was on her way
        To defeat the one who orphaned her that day.

7: The Sandstorm

Prince Akbar's illness caused the harbor to be guarded round the clock.
A quarantine prevented ships from anchoring and sailing from the dock.
Nevertheless, Victoria bought a camel and, taking its reins in hand,
Set out into the desert, which was desolate except for sand.
As Victoria and her camel left the city's gate,
Both Ramfalcis and Doldrum hid in wait.
When the ramparts disappeared from her gaze,
The two wretched demons started a craze.
Ramfalcis threw so much sand up in the air
That to current day some spots still lay bare.
When Doldrum's turn came to harass the dame,
His laziness won, and the winds became tame.
Think like a snow-globe in hand of a child.
She gives it a shake, and the powder goes wild.
So that when shaken, the scene disappears.
After the powder settles, it soon reappears.
So too the mighty sandstorm had its way
That Vicky knew not if it was night or day.
Covering her eyes, she said a quick prayer:
That God would kindly lead her out of there.
Hearing this, He sent her a worthy guide.
A blackbird landed in a tree near the castle's side.
The bird then sang above the sandstorm's attack.
And Vicky, eyes closed, guided her camel back.

8: The Alchemist
Fire
Air
Earth
Water

Knowing not how to progress, she began to cry
When along came a most kind, friendly Rabbi.
The Rabbi sat down and quieted her sobbing,
Asking if Victoria was a victim of a robbing.
She shook her head and explained her plight.
He suspected not storm but demons in flight.
To an oasis Vicky was directed by the helpful Rabbi
To obtain a golden shield from an alchemist nearby.
Once a mighty, errant knight in his early life,
Now only herbs know the sting of his knife.
Francis was his name of the crest Blackbird.
His legendary exploits even Vicky had heard.
He seemed to wander throughout every country,
Performing daring feats in the name of chivalry.
But, during the crusade, he witnessed such sin
And quit when he saw knights butcher children.
These memories always bring him much sorrow,
But his flask brings him comfort until tomorrow.
He sold his armor and sword – but not his shield! –
For various scrolls pertaining to the alchemical field.
The art was the method of God, they say.
It's how He created life in a single day.
The foolish try to make gold transmuted from lead
While the sagely person sees it as a metaphor instead:
Our fleshy body is the lead like the cacoon of a butterfly,
And the gold that emerges is the soul, which can never die.
Now, Francis settled in the oasis right outside of the wall
And practiced his occult craft for the great benefit of all.
Vicky approached him telling of the Rabbi.
She asked for help, which he did not deny.
Using the properties of earth, fire, water, and air,
Francis strengthened his old shield for one so fair.
This shield was imbued with a blessed light.
It could ward off evil and the darkest night.

9: The Final Battle

Francis joined her saying his art might come in handy.
In truth the thought of adventure seemed just dandy.
The demons blew up the storm just as before,
Thinking the girl would retreat once more.
She rode with the shield high above her head.
When the light hit the demons, each one fled.
Then, Vicky was truly able to start on her quest.
The pair rode for ten days with minimal rest.
Dismounting, the pair quietly walked to the gate.
She told her old friend outside he should wait.
She wondered, as she entered the castle to face her foe,
If she would come out alive - she honestly did not know.
When Eladrin saw her, his laugh was cold:
Surely his frail niece could not be so bold.
She threw her spear as he shouted a spell.
They passed in midair, only one ending well.
His chanted spell echoed with quite a clamor
And struck her shield like a mighty hammer.
Although it protected her, Victoria still went flying.
Behold! Her spear hit its mark, who now lay dying.
Eladrin yanked the spear from his bleeding breast,
And his black heart toppled from his gaping chest.
He watched his cursed heart give a final beat.
Then, the magic scepter shattered with his defeat.

10: The Dragon

Ba'al chuckled, as he watched wretched Eladrin die,
And entered his body for the end was not yet nigh.
His body twitched and contorted as if under attack!
Then leathery, black wings sprouted from his back.

His body elongated to the size of a whale
And ended in a barbed, serpentine tail.
Twisted horns like a goat's grew from his head.
'Twas lucky for Eladrin that he was already dead.
With a gnarled, clawed foot it crushed the spear.
Now our brave Victoria had reason to truly fear.

Hearing the ruckus and roars from the outside,
The unarmed alchemist dared to venture inside.
Seeing Vicky sprawled defenseless on floor,
Courage called his spirit to action once more.
He stepped between her and Ba'al without fear.
The dragon breathed deep and started to rear.

As you watched your doom, you did not even blink.
All you did was slowly uncork your wine filled drink.
You, who knew the secrets to never face death,
Saved Vicky's life by blocking that fiery breath.
Francis, I swear your name shall never die!
Your fame will be sung by angels on high!
Victoria watched her burnt friend fall at her feet.
Wiping away her tears, she swore never to retreat.

11: A Heavenly Hand

Way up high on the fluffy clouds above,
A mother tore her face in anguished love.
Ann ran frantically through the golden street
And threw herself down at her savior's feet.
"My Lord, all my life I followed your way
So that I might find peace in Heaven one day.
But even here and now my tears continue to flow
Because I'm distraught by the events down below.
My sweet daughter, Victoria, faces wicked Ba'al,
Before whom even glorious angels sometimes fall.
Snatch her away safely, is all that I ask,
Or send aid for such a dangerous task.
Recall Mary's pain as you hung on the cross.
Spare my motherly heart such a similar loss."
Having stirred memories in His great heart,
Jesus helped her up and a speech did start:
"Please, dear woman, hold back your sad tears.
Father plans she will live for many more years.
But snatch her from the fight this cannot be.
She must stop wicked Ba'al to fulfill destiny.
Now a holy sword to her Rafael will give.
Its powers shall ensure Victoria will live."
Rafael took flight at the Lord's command
With a demon-slaying sword in his hand.
He found Victoria holding up just a shield.
Not even the dragon could make her yield.
Rafael left the divine sword at Victoria's feet.
Then back towards heaven his wings did beat.

12: A Legendary Tale

Ba'al reared his hideous head back for a final blast
While Vicky charged with her new sword held fast.
A second later, Victoria would have been smote,
But the sword slit the demonic dragon's throat.
The flames shot out and melted off its ugly face.
With the dragon now dead, Ba'al fled in disgrace.
Shakily, heroic Victoria wiped the ash from her dome
And surveyed the damage done to her ancestral home.
Beware! For the devil had but one last trick.
He shook the land, and the castle fell quick.
Our hero would have been crushed – a sad tale to tell! –
But luckily for us, she knew her familial castle well.
Victoria ducked into a secret chamber and huddled inside,
Where during games her brother, Henry, used to hide.
When Vicky emerged from her humble hiding place,
The ancient, grand castle was gone without a trace.
But seeing this our hero Vicky did not lose heart.
She gathered all her people, and repairs they did start.
Soon Burgess Kingdom even surpassed its former glory.
Thus, happily concludes Queen Victoria's legendary story.

Want to read more from the world of *Agrey's Fables*®?

Use your smartphone camera to scan the QR Code:

Or, I guess, just type it in the old-fashioned way:

www.agreys-fables.com